HOME FOR

HURRICANES

*a memoir of resilience
in poetry and prose*

NIKKI MURPHY

REBIЯTH
PRESS
Freeport, NY

The events and conversations in this book have been set down to the best of the author's ability. This story is based on actual events, though the author has taken certain creative liberties with metaphors and chronology for poetic effect.

First Edition 2020

Book illustration by Rafael Faustino

Library of Congress Control Number: 2020917174

ISBN 978-1-7353879-0-1 (paperback)
ISBN 978-1-7353879-1-8 (ebook)

www.nikki-murphy.com

For my younger self
my children and their children
and anyone weathering a storm.
You were built to withstand.

CONTENTS

HOME FOR
HURRICANES

HOME

ALL HONOR TO THE LIFE-GIVERS

For Black women
who while treading water
nestled brick men and dough babies
on bosoms unproud
stood target for bullets
misfired and loud

to daring daughters
of flighty fathers
who laid down
their bare bodies
to be slaughtered
spotting love's twinkle
in every lustful glance
and after bloodied betrayals
again
granted love a chance

there's no payment sufficient
to honor your worth;
most astounding creation
you—the face of this earth

On the Seventh Day We Could Not Rest

It was 1986
before seats were belted
before smoke could be secondhand
before we breathed
in words of caution and regret
Nana drove my laboring mother
to the hospital of good Samaritans.

At twenty
my mother
or I
or the world between us
was not yet ready to break.

It was the morning of the seventh day
of the month of pearls and divergent twins.
Saturday, a single man
knifed a gate
through chain-link fencing.

Saturday, seven pounds
of life lifted
from her unlatched womb.
Saturday was an emergency
surgery stapled shut.

But we survived

Saturday

My mother and I.

BOW-BOWS & BARRETTES

Black and
Blue Magic
in black girls'
hair fabric
kinks magic
elastic
our backs
gold-fastened
plastic
balls,
beads,
barrettes
like pom-poms,
we bring
our own
pep

to the rally.

And blood.
And bone.
And dance.
For our lives.

I Used To

In the street, street girls dance night and day,
choreography made with ease.
Our tape records the radio's cries;
I used to have hobbies.

A dance contest, I dared to enter
caving to family's pleas.
Slashed my opponents with bogle back bend—
brought them to their knees.

Made rugs of yarn with one latch hook
weaved to interlock;
hung the wall art of colored strings
as pictured on the box.

A pot to hold my siphoned concoctions
heaven-scented potions—
a scientist's theory to be tested
with mom's perfumes and lotions.

Jeans cut short meant extra fabric
I gather she might fit
with needle and thread, I stitch unhemmed
a Barbie doll outfit.

To write of places unseen, people unknown
made no bit of difference
I'd pen a plot twist, love letter, or poem.
Mom smiled at every sentence.

Zig-zag parts drawn to one side—
asymmetric ponytail
I'd cornrow a crown of yours or mine
a braided fairytale.

I used to have hobbies, then I had track practice
'cause college didn't consider
the hobbies undocumented as a child
exactly extracurricular.

Now I had to run from school to practice,
practice on to work.
From there, back home to lay on my mattress
with noodles, bowl, and fork.

I used to have hobbies, but high school, then college
where I had to choose
only one interest of all the options;
just one I could pursue.

My day is jam-packed from beginning to end,
still found time to party,
if only for a dorm room fête to know
life still in my body.

I used to have hobbies some years ago
still kinda held on to one.
But braiding guys' hair straight back for money
wasn't creative or fun.

I used to have a hobby of sorts
until I got a career;
working long hours for people in power
in a heat with all of my peers.

Changing diapers, clothes and cooking supper–
the hobbies of wives and mothers.
Any free time is for a drink on the couch
or TV to recover

Some people have hobbies, but just not me;
there's no time for that.
Besides, anything I loved, I never mastered, so
nothing I'm good at.

My dancing and braiding still lives inside
a mediocre life at best.
I only sew now to mend a split
torn while sitting to rest.

My pen is for to-do-lists, notes, reminders
or to journal my trauma.
The only potions I mix are coffee with milk
or a drink– cranberry & vodka.

A Haiku for Renaissance Children

I want to be a
scientist – model – dancer
do not make me choose

A HAIKU FOR SINGLE MOTHER & CHILD

Emptied bags of trust
Mommy and me carry on
store window shopping

WATERING CEMENT

My family is no comforter;
they don't fold and bend.

They are
>**cement**–
>graffiti-laced walls
>returning bullets
>Strong. Tough. Towering.

But I
>I am not **cement**
>I am *water*, rushing
>to be made solid.

MOMMY SHOWS ME BETTER THAN SHE CAN TELL ME

My mommy loves me.
She says so in enough words
like "want to come to the store
with me?"
Let's me ride shotgun
in the murky
blue Corsica that reeks
of spoiled milk in summer.
At the mall, I fawn over
dessert displays
but do not drool.
We've already had the talk
in the parking lot
several times before.
I recite it with her
leaving blanks
where her cusses fall,
"I don't see _____.
I don't want _____.
I ain't getting _____."
She laughs.
And I don't ask.
I am the good child.
Her only child.

After dinner, I pull my chair and chest
into the wood kitchen table,
my back to the hallway (lest I be
distracted by the bustle
of the evening—
other kids, elders, family)

and swallow all the back pages
of the dictionary—a gift from my mother
for one of the two gift-giving holidays.
I memorize states and their capitals,
though I'll never be tested by anyone
other than her.
Juneau is like June,
my birth month,
which is opposite of the cold
Alaska.
Mommy dresses in pride
under her employer-issued burgundy
vest before she leaves for work.

My mother is Black.
Everything she owns tells me
so. She makes me love being
Black too. She buys me books
and lets me read about smart girls—
like Addy and later, Winter—
that survived slavery and the ghetto,
respectively.
I imagine them both my friends.
American girls.
American girl heroes.
My American girl heroes.

When mommy goes to the store
for work, I rewind
and rewatch *Soul Food*
I gather that I am more Bird than Teri
though all these ladies show me
pain is inevitable. Love is all that matters
really.

And hair.

I can't get a perm.
Mommy says *no,*
you're gonna look your age
even though we both wear
a size 10 shoe now.
She washes, blows, combs,
and braids my hair.
Even at my height, she spins me 'round
and makes me cower
down on the floor
between her legs
to braid upward.
I am still her child.
Beads rattle against their tin prison
in protest, on my behalf.

Mommy is thirty now.
Everyone in middle school says
we look like sisters.
"Your mom must be so cool!"
I roll my eyes.
Mommy says "I am not
one of your little friends,"
then, walks me to the bus stop
to see which one of these heifers
got somethin' to say.
I am hot with embarrassment.
My mother fought my battle.

Which is more than I could say
about Winter's mother.

SOMETHIN' TO CRY ABOUT

look up chile
stop being so sensitive
sticks and stones

sticks and stones

if somebody hit you
tell the teacher
if somebody hit you
whup they ass

whup they ass

stop walking round here wit' an attitude
you don't pay no bills
I'll give you somethin' to cry about

I'll give you somethin' to cry about...

WITHOUT QUESTION

A bird without yet magic in its wings
dropped from its nest. The boys
burned it alive. Singed, I screamed vapor
and turned to hide silent   tears that apologize
for boys who take what they want
without question.

Thieving boy lips branded my dimple. Cooties
crawled. In first grade, I felt my first kiss. And cried
"Teacher!" till giggles flew around
teacher's pencil sharpened teeth. My kind
of pretty baited parasites.

Daddy's never home
but his grandmother holds my chin
up and tells me *"you're so pretty."*
And my mom.
She will have to watch out
for the boys. I thought she meant
their eyes.

But they stuck their
stubby fingers in my Wednesday
panties. When the bus door opened
its mouth to stop traffic, it was the breathing
that started

the ugly cry
that summoned principals
and parents to my living room
to apologize for boys who take
what they want
without question
and tell me to
speak up.

FORBIDDEN FRUIT IS STILL FRUIT

Dancing
Smiling
Laughing
Hula hooping
Street cheers
Sleepovers
Rolling on lip gloss

Like the apple
From the all-wise tree,
Things I loved were cursed

When I did them in front of boys.

BLACK BOY LAUGHS MUSIC TO MY EARS

Black boy laughs reverberate
                off walls and breaks them.
The Black boy laughs under pressure.

Black boy laughs axe
                whole train cars underground.
The Black boy laughs barricades.

Black boy laughs turn bass drum.
                Familiar faces catch the rhythm.
The Black boy laughs a beat.

Waiting for the other

                                to drop…

The silence is deadly.

FOR ROMAN

it was a nice campus
but the flowers
seemed a little too bright
the other students in the program
a little too white
then I spotted you

us, two teens from the same school
in a lab with goggles, burners, real science tools
an experiment, the subjects: me and you
taken out of our element to learn something new
adapting, pouring solution from a beaker to a flask
and when I needed help, I didn't even have to ask
bonding, we learned how opposites attract
how when separated
magnetic force would pull them right back

when we left, I didn't have your number
and you didn't have mine
after school, I went to college
and you…
you stayed behind

the next time I'd see you
6 years, far too late
you'd be dressed to kill

and I'd be at your wake.

And all the article's comments would paint a distorted
   picture
that somehow your life was deserving of that trigger
trolls telling the world how much they hate our town
how they can't drive through so they gotta drive around
how they wished that we'd all just kill each other
a murder in March, damn
it ain't even summer

I wanted to respond and tell them about the guy I knew
how it was all about the team and never once about you
I wanted to respond and tell them
about the guy you used to be
how you loved to joke around and smile more than me
and how you'd measure the liquid filling in the glass
apply heat, sit back smiling, waiting for the gas
how you were so polite on that ride home with my mother
how you never even missed a single session that summer

I hate that in your death
your life was misunderstood
where I saw a smiling scientist,
they saw a thug
from the hood

I know that a sinner can be forgiven
so I pray that you're in a lab room in heaven
maybe it was you that caused that last thunderstorm,
that rainbow, or day that was a little too warm

perhaps you're petitioning for every dope boy and trap queen
asking God to shine a light on the rock
and hard place they're stuck in between.
while you're up there talking with Him,
I'll be down here trying to change the world from within

sometimes I wonder how things would have been
if maybe after high school, you enrolled at UPenn
and studied math or science,
why the rain drops from a cloud
then come back to the hood and make everybody proud

I wish I would've told you what the counselors told me
how things could be different if you get a degree
how sometimes you have to leave your comfort zone
and go away
even if it means leaving mom at home
alone

until now I didn't notice how your death affected me
how in the same year that you died, I started mentoring
now I go into schools without laboratories
and tell the kids about the power in their stories
record 'em on a track, act it out in a play,
type it up and submit it as a college essay
they smile like you
because they have something to say
to change the world
we gotta fight in more than one way

so I tell the kids that college is poppin'
and how even with no money, they still got a few options
though it seems you're signing up for years of strife
a student loan is a small price to pay for a life
so I enroll a kid in a college course
this is how I channel my survivor's remorse

for a second I understand why things had to be this way
why you had to go, why I had to stay
look at you

started a revolution
and you ain't even know it
your blood's the ink in the pen,
moved by a poet
our story
I'll put it in a poem
For Roman.
a soldier
shot
on his way home

9/11 IN HOOD CLASSROOMS

Prologue:
When one of us died,
school was still in session.

The world spun
around the nerves,
around the *damn, shit-crazy's*,
around jump ropes and shots.
Around us, school bells scream.

We pop seals of fire alarms like soda cans
to drink fresh air.

Feature:

Nine-Eleven–a foreign tragedy sans
subtitles, we watched
innocent people die.
Class ceased.

The world choked
around the nerves,
around the soot-stained bodies,
around the damning devastation.
Around them, even school bells
scream.

Teachers begged us to care.
To stop talking over their grief—

the way they taught us.

CLOSETS

SHACKLED STORIES

prisoners of my mind
overcrowded
with hope
for early release

THINGS I LEARNED IN BOOT CAMP FOR INDEPENDENT WOMEN

1.   How to stand alone, solid

2.   To pay my own way, so it's clear
     I don't owe you anything

3.   To lift a car, remove the bolts and change
     its tires

4.   I can do everything you can

     Except

     Love me

PRIVILEGE IN THE YEAR OF AALIYAH

To be
young
pretty
top of my class
light-skinned
dimpled
responsible
tall
slender
timid
long-haired
and undeniably

unlovable.

What is this life
if only a body
of desire?

THE MODEST CONVERSION

At 16, the pressure circles my unveiled body.

I am single (without protection) and it seems every guy, street and saint, wants. I am too embarrassed to blame my mother's rules, to explain that there are rules, and approvals, and supervision, and judgements (not mine).

Islam came, not in my babysitter's storefront sanctuary where convulsion seized my body against a wooden pew—an encounter that moved me to confess Jesus as my Lord and Savior two years and heartbreaks prior—but just as obvious.

Islam's rules were a picture of what I could be: more beauty than bleary, more logical than emotional, more lawful, less forgiving. Having worked for everything else, it seemed salvation should be no different.

At 16, I am tired of falling for nothing.

Hijab be a covering. Mask the parts that entice. Render me exotic and off market. Quell the lust.

Islam be a standard for boys to approach me only with the intent to marry. Finally. Serious inquiries only.

I am serious too.

I study, wash, pray.
Memorize, wash, pray.
Take a new name (Sanaa), wash, pray.
Learn the Arabic alphabet, wash, pray.
Tell my mother I am not in a cult (my brain is the
only thing that has not been washed), wash, pray.
Eat halal (mostly), wash, pray.
Go to Jum'ah some Fridays, wash, pray.
Find sisterhood with breathtakingly beautiful girls,
wash, pray.
Ask the manager for a break, wash, pray.
Tell my mom I don't believe that one's family could
be Christian by default. Why does my religion
matter anymore than the lack thereof? Wash, pray.
Give salaams, wash, pray.

And learn
Muslim boys
are boys
nonetheless.

DTP

The doorbell chimes
a sweet
sounding
reminder
that you are here

to disturb the peace.

WARNING LABELS

He, a tall glass.
Drink responsibly. Ignore.
Know your limit. Ignore.
Indulge at your own risk. Ignore.

Why is the warning always written in *fine* print?

CHILDREN PLAY WITH LOVE

Children play with love
at first sight, they squeeze it tight
straighten its legs
and drown it in swimming pools.

Children play with love
bounce it up and down
back and forth it's thrown
up and laughed at.

Children play with love
step in its hollow
spin it round their neck
and waist, and hips, and feet.

Children play with love
turn it on and on and on
drain its batteries
and bang a dead thing.

Children play with love
put it in a box, turn handles
all around the Mulberry bush
children pop love.

And close their eyes.
And count to ten.
Then, say it again,

I (would) love (for) you

        (to

            chase

                me).

LOVE STORMS

Loving you is like
loving a hurricane
with its unpredictable path
at the last minute

you'll turn...

DEAR DIARY, I'M HAVING A PANIC ATTACK

My mind
tried to kill me last night.

I know it doesn't make sense
because you don't know
how this feels
like the last time
that was like the last time
that was like the first time

he left me. The devil
ignites tears,
tantrums, wild
punches, a radical escape
from everyone.
There is just me

and my mind trying to kill
the object I worshipped—a façade.
Stupid!
The Wiz was just a man.
Stupid!
And I just a fan.
Stupid.
God, I wish I was home.

IDENTITY CRISIS

I was a flower
until you told me
I was brown

and there are no brown flowers.

BEFORE I SHUT THE DOOR

death
came close
to home
today

I Don't Mean It

No one calls to say

I'm leaving

        unless they want a hand

to pull them back.

CAN ANYBODY HEAR ME?

If I were cut at the ankles and barreled down

>would my plummet make a sound?

If I let men make beds in my hollow

>would the waking stirs of love soon follow?

If I red-stickered my soul and marked it clearance

>would that suffice as repentance?

If I leaned into the rushing waves of hope

>would God toss me a saving rope?

HURRICANES

DADDY'S CONFESSION

I remember the day my daddy confessed. I was a post-college adult, in the backseat of a car with both my reunited and newly introduced half siblings–the partition between my whole father and I. Am priest in the way that I absorb the unfiltered confessions of my then chronically ill and spiritually transformed father. He reflects on his life, not knowing that it would be over in five short years.

First, he warned, "you'll probably hate me for this." Then, without a pause to even momentarily debate sharing, he confessed. Sins against desperate women. *If there was anything to hate you for, might it have been the years of my life that you were absent? Not how you filled your time.*

Besides, I couldn't imagine it. Sure, he walked the neighborhood with a black and gold cane, gold rings on every finger, not to be overshadowed by the layers of gold chains donned around his neck like anchors. And years, dressed in one loud color from head to toe, topped with a Kangol hat for good measure; yes, he looked the part. And people joked of it. Still, it was hard to read intimidation when he always beamed a shining, dumbfounded gold-toothed grin whenever he saw me, which was mostly every second Saturday in June—Wyandanch Day—when I walked over to him in the park and introduced myself, "hey."

I'd pause uncomfortably for a few seconds while he tried to place where he knew me from. At my breaking point, "It's Nikki." Then, there it was, that wide, toothy grin and open embrace, like I was an unexpected Amazon package arriving on his doorstep without his recalling having ordered just the thing he'd been looking for. His not knowing me upon initial greeting was a running joke between my homegirl and I. We would laugh about it afterward (in the way that teenagers laugh off the things that should hurt them). That unquick, cheesing grin made it hard to imagine him a threat to anyone.

He continued with stories about ex-lovers, about the violence, about getting run over by a car—the accident that resulted in extensive brain damage, causing him to have to relearn and remember many things, including that he had me.

This accident hung over our relationship, or lack thereof, like a grey cloud unsure of whether to rain or run. Is the accident the reason he never recognized me? *Or* was it because he was never there? Was he not there because he didn't remember his connection to me? *Or* did he remember and choose to ignore my existence (until we ran into each other in the neighborhood and did this song and dance about how proud he was of me and how pretty I was)?

I don't know. But I swallowed his confessions (about everything but the obvious) like manna from heaven because it was something. To know about my father.

That he recognized his unproud moments. And he remembered.

It would take me awhile, years even, to understand that his karma found me. Even when he did not.

COLLEGE

It's been said
you meet your husband
here on campus
you can be new
and improved
subtract and omit
the things you are
add and embellish
the things you wish
you were
and there

the love of your life
will find you
dancing in brand new
freedom
a brand new
woman

keep both eyes open
don't rule anyone out
college is full
of potential

DORM ROOM ESSENTIALS

- Twin XL sheets
- Computer
- Corkboard
- Pictures of
    1. the tribe of women that conspired to bring you here
    2. the friends you don't want to forget
    3. you, doing something interesting
- Notebooks
- Pens
- Mace

ME AND MY GIRLS

We exchange compliments,
laugh at magazine pics,
professors, girls, and boys.

We belt lyrics loudly
and to each other
in the middle of dance floors.

Hips sway in sync till
your favorite part plays;
then I step back
and let you shine,
"Go girl, go girl!
That's my best friend!"
You do the same on mine.

ALTER EGO

If I were a man-eating man-eater
I'd snack on men *so fine*
often, I'd rot my sweetest tooth
and crown the hole left behind.

If I were a man-eating man-eater
I'd prefer them wild caught
fished from trucks and clubs myself
fresher than those bought.

If I were a man-eating man-eater
I'd take them medium rare
with soft bleeding hearts, I'd tear apart
and leave no fat to spare.

If I were a man-eating man-eater
I'd feast three meals a day
with malty drinks of bottled tears
to wash the longing away.

If I were a man-eating man-eater
my stomach would ache so bad
I'd curse every bone, "Leave me alone"
and wonder... who really got had?

Even Then, Enough Is Enough

my sexy floats around
like carbon monoxide
in the bedroom

don't know why
but you can't stop
falling

even when I say

enough

FRIENDS WITH BENEFITS OF DOUBT

Under the heat
my frozen body melted
tears; you claimed
not to have noticed.

Like an iron
to a stubborn wrinkle
you imagined
I wanted to be made flat.

Hadn't I invited myself
atop the ironing board
and looked up, teasingly?

I didn't know you were serious.
You should have hit me harder.
I thought you meant "stop" like girls do.

Of course,
just a misunderstanding.
Friends don't hurt each other.
And if we are friends, I am not hurt.

These are the lies we tell ourselves
to cope.

URBANIZATION

You steamrolled over
    the speed bumps on my skin.

You plowed every
    tall standing, carefree part of me.

You dug up
    a bright garden and poured grey concrete.

You wielded a rifle
    and did that killer move

until I played dead.
    If only dead bodies cried

for their tragic ending.

RUIN

Ruin

A

Person

Egregiously

Bring Back the Life of the Party

bring the herb, 151, a party
to make me forget
bring the big and small jokers
deuces, paper, pen
bring dancehall, soca and whine

bring laughs, always the laughs
Lil' Kim lyrics even when you are out
your mind you are hardcore
bring Devil Springs
bring 151 and chalk
make me forget

blackout

outline
the shell of me
dancing in bullseyes
crashing on floors

find the clues
(laugh)
arrows hidden
(dance)
under my skirt
(lyrics)
bring me my skirt
(mind)
make me forget

blackout

the big and small

jokers
made
a shell
of me

forget

GOD WATCHED A GANG...

Hang me from a crane,

    six
    stories,

        like
        I
        asked

            for
            it.

SIDE EFFECTS

I am stained
when my body is naked; it is black,
draped with the heavy curtain of confusion,
floating atop the raft of your lies,
swaying in waves of nausea.
I am back home—

sick.

Oak

Even   shame me
    the   to
      trees   tall

          stand

A CRUCIFIX

I wonder…

> Whose sin I'm paying for?
> Whose coarse curse curled itself
> around my fighting parts,
> and lynched them to the bed?
> How do I stomp the serpent on its head?
>
> With my resurrection?

…I wonder.

CAST YOUR CARES

I held my guilt
like cornmeal
like drumsticks
like flour
like potatoes
like macaroni
like sharp and mild cheddar
like soul

food in grocery bags
ten to an arm
I am not coming back.

HOLD IT TOGETHER

I am angry. Then, I am numb.
I am angry. Then, I am fun.
I am angry.
I am angry.
I am angry!

I guess you won.

MY BODY FEELS ANCIENT

Like the rough
centuries-old weeping trees,
thick, twisted roots
remember everything.
My body feels
a n c i e n t.

EVEN THE EARTH QUAKES

It is you that still causes me
to spring to the top of my headboard
feet bicycle against the unexpected arrival
of my true love's touch.

I am ticklish.
But it is not funny.
I could hurt
for what I can't separate.
This is not danger.
He is not you.
I beg a break.

To breathe.
And take.
Control.

HURRICANES

every hurricane must be named
so you don't soon forget
destruction is never anonymous

REBUILDING

WHETHER OR NOT

It is all I have
left to hold on to
the fact that God
loves me.

Whether I read
the holy word
or not.
Sing hallelujah praise
or not.
Perform on stages
or in private rooms
or not.

Whether I smile when
all that is
within me
cries.
Whether I am stone when
all that is
within me
sands.
Weather sunny
or rain
storms.

Whether I have
a good job
money
cars

health
or not.
Whether I am building
the country
or burning
it down.
Especially when
I am burning it down.

Whether they call
me "baby girl"
or "bitch"
or tell me
what I think
I am.
I think I am
loved.

Whether I flip the table
or play the hand,
I am loved
even when
I cannot
deal.

You're Gonna Make It

Writhing in pain
for twelve rotting days

clinging to sayings
of embracing this phase

of loads we can carry
like stink in our hair

of wages of sin
and crosses to bear

of how He knew my life
before it began

and how even the worst things
work out in the end.

RHYTHM & BUSTLE

The pulse of the beat
plucks me from my bed
of misery, moving my feet
one after the other
in sync. I percolate perfectly
against this percussion
masked in a plastered smile.
New York City's upbeat tempo
peaks perpetually.
Piles of hours burn
till ceremony's close.

Slow down.

TWENTY-FIVE

1.

I don't know why
I am working
the job I am
but I am good
at it

2.

I am single
have been
for months
it is the only
thing I didn't just
fall into

3.

I have my own
place and car
matchbox and rusted
and mine
alone

4.

For my birthday
I buy makeup, hair, wardrobe
bottle service
friends
we are celebrating
a quarter century
of survival

5.

I am drunk
and bruised
when I am sober
single is still
the only thing I have
not fallen into

I Kept Going

I saw a man get away with it
And put my own vision on trial
I hid with chattering girls in bedroom closets
I cut my wrist on a lie
I picked a scab until it bled
I washed
And rewashed
I held my own hand and prayed
I cut my hair and dyed it red
I took a shot
I wrote a novel, a mystery
Ripped the pages
I started a fire and watched it burn
I blew ashes
I built a business
And tore it down
I carried a baby
Twice
I stubbed my toe and cracked concrete
I stood in a pool of blood
I broke my knees on hardwood floors
I remembered
I banged my head and begged it to stop
I laughed a belly laugh
I cut my hair
Again
I posted a selfie
And counted my likes
I packed a baseball bat, pepper spray, bags

My car shut off
Twice
In traffic, I broke down

I balanced a pail of water on my head
Upside down, I nearly drowned
Open mouthed,
I caught the ocean
Sigh

I crawled to work and raised my hand
I tasted a man
Then swallowed him whole
My belly aches
I stopped eating pork
I dreamt of fortune and slept with mice
I tasted dirt
My tears salted the earth

I surrendered.

A Prodigal Daughter's Living Sacrifice

Hope,
lie me on the altar
in my someday best.
Leave me. Waiting.

Are you still there?
Do you still hear?

I am believing

in resurrection.

WORK IN PROGRESS

Survival is selfish
I've survived too
I've forgiven hurt men like you.

But me,
I should've known
what I couldn't have known
in the condition my knowing was in.

I'm working on it... freedom.

AVOIDING SUSPICION

When I run
scorching water and scrub the stubborn scum

I daydream of asking more questions
to the ladies in my life

questions that keep curling into balls at the base
of my throat

questions that tell about the bones
I carry, the haunting

questions that exclamation point
to black bruises beneath the *good, and you?*

questions that pound like battering
rams to shut doors

questions that won't ever be answered
honestly because it feels like something
to forget

questions that won't ever be asked
honestly, I promise I am not
~~fine~~ guilty

THERE'S NO CURE FOR TRAUMA POX

My tied hands carefully place pink chamomile lotion
and concoct luxurious spa baths of lukewarm water
and old-fashioned oats, in peeling tubs and sanitizing solitude
till torment fades into dark scars, only where I entertained
the inviting itch of it.

The virus lies dormant, making a cozy cottage
of my cured enough body, threatening
to resurface, later, unexpectedly

and in new form, worse with age and knowing
a full free life, grown in relative bliss
with many branches donning succulent fruit

and

shingles.

HASHTAG

I hate
the words
for how they
air a hidden flame:

me too.

PREPARING FOR TAKEOFF

On behalf of the flight crew, we would like to
welcome you aboard Opportunity Flight 1111.

We have a full flight today.

We are looking for a few volunteers to check their
trauma at the gate.

We need you, standing in the aisle, to come back to
the front and check your trauma.

Be sure to unzip your trauma and take out anything
you need for the journey.

Sir, the overhead compartment is full.
Ma'am, it will not fit.

We need you to loosen your grip on the trauma. We
would be happy to assist.

Please follow our direction. Or you and your
trauma will be forcibly removed.

We want to take off and get you to your destination
safely.

Our goal is an on-time arrival.

Are you willing to let go?

BLACK RESPONSIBILITY

Like the old me, she is frail.
And innocent.
And I don't trust her
to carry the weight—
my porcelain therapist.

Until the Thursday that *I* broke.

She folds forward,
wide laser beaming eyes
cut and console me,
they were wrong for what they did to you.
I don't disagree.
But I don't absolve myself.

I should have turned back
to make certain that
the iron was unplugged,
car doors locked and my purse
not carelessly left in plain sight.
That I did not forget the baby
in the backseat.

That, at home, my long robe was shut
with a tight knot for the family men.
That I made momma secure
my beads with rubber bands
not foil that slips
into catastrophe.
That I did everything I could
to prevent this house fire.

Or at least, not fan the flame.

That I am not the pot.
Calling the kettle.

ONE WISH

I want everyone
to be less and
more responsible
than I was.

POST-TRAUMATIC STAGE FRIGHT MANTRA

Everybody is nobody at all.

Everybody is nobody at all.

Everybody is nobody at all.

Everybody is nobody.

HIP HOP TAUGHT ME

Some days I wear
my pride like
ten gold chains with
ten gold rings like
daddy used to do.

Bass blasting, I stand
erect, belting beside
billionaire's buildings,
bow down bitches!

A NEW DAY

One day you will
wake with no tears to shed,
not for empty wells, but for
evaporation turning overflowing pain
into overflowing rain—
nature's course
for growing.

SELF-CARE IN SUMMER

I dine at nice establishments
that play my music
on occasion
saxophones hook
me and make me feel
almost naked
I boycott coffee
some days
it seems
I should will myself awake
and sit in my life
sober

I rub sand over my skin to shed
the dull and bathe
in saltwater beaches
the sun does not burn me
it loves me
sore

I don't want for anything
it is already mine

SALVATION

Behind the curtain, we cry
a prayer that screams
like "Help!"

At our brazen call, All That Is
God shifts the tide
of war.

By the lure of victory, we dream
a new vision
for our lives.

That is to say
the God in us created
a new life
from the burning
ruins of old.

Nothing is wasted.

I LIVE

I see a vision for my life.

I am the child of God
therefore, I create the world
I live in.

I decide
what I will take
and not.
I decide
what will kill
my spirit
or shake it
awake.

I own my own body
and my own life.
More than that,
I love them
dearly. They carried me,
the gift of them,
through it all.

I am more than
an incident
a rape
an insult
or several.

They never had the power
to define me

I have come to collect
the debts
and forgive
those that have trespassed.

I am the child of God.
I create
the world.
I live.

EXPANDING

I breathed deep and loud
took up space
I grew three inches.

I told loud stories
in crowded restaurants.
I cussed.
I waited.
I cussed again.
I asked for the waiter two, no
three times
whenever I needed
I grew three inches.

I ate all the dishes I liked
with peach cobbler, vanilla
ice cream and glass
I grew three inches.

I wrapped my hands
around the shaft
of a microphone
and spoke my truth
I grew three inches.

CHANGING WINDS

the moment is clear
all the events of my life
blew together
and chimed in my ear
something's here

when did sitting atop
unsought dreams become so
popular?
clothe me in urgency
feed me the rush.
the gold. the waterfall.
the boundless waves
with their frothy edge.
feed me rush.

keep the piano out of this.
my heart won't be strung out.
feed me bass drums
and foot stomps
and howls to Oshun.
I'm birthing a miracle. baby,
feed me the womb.

through the trees, the breeze
burns like sizzle.
the moment is clear.
all the events of my life
blew together
and chimed in my ear.
something's here.

INVESTMENT

With the slightest hope of this
day my ancestors endured.

I too persist

for descendants unknown, yet
sense I gained much more.

Hair (R)evolution

Great-gran   parted
the Black   Sea
and   braided
two   bodies.

Nana
        lowered
the tide
        with
one
        pointing
finger
        waved
the
        ocean to
and fro

Momma
laid
whole
hands
on
the
dreaded
ocean
and
rolled it
in her
palms.

Me,   I   set   it   free.

EXONERATED

please accept
the apology
from your future
self.

you were
never too much
never not enough
only too hard
on you.

so much more
than what happened
when your glisten
whet appetites
of savages
who needed
to devour

everyone fighting
their own
demons
can't apologize
and mean it.
you do.

for all the mean
things you said
when you were
on a platter,
knife and fork
pressed to your throat.

live.

and let
the record show:

though you
were bruised
in conflict
you are
no less
diamond.

BLESS YOU

Loudly, I bless each generation
of valor and siphoned reparations,
of hustle, shots, of separation,
of crippling blows and stoutly sobs,
of men entitled and others robbed.

MAN THAT FEELS LIKE HOME

(Can be read column by column or straight across)

your eyes	betray your stoic demeanor
brightly lit lenses	take in the world
filter	through your heart
light only	don't burn out

your nature	ever
shows in casual interactions,	*you*–an uncommon life raft
not brightly colored but	impossible to overlook
strong, powerful, solid	a reflection of God's own love

a new testament to	your old story–sacrifice
your body,	accentuated by scars
the remnants of	a tragedy averted
a battle	for your life's purpose
heaven's inscriptions	on smooth, brown skin
pain was here, life transformed	*new life begins*

sealed lips part	a bridge
once	appearing fixed, now draws
a smile	and ships set sail

love	trailing
strength	fueling
vision	guiding

home

WILL YOU MARRY ME?

He risks cutting
his lips against the jagged
edges of my heart.
He came to call me his
love.

I weighed the title
in both hands
then pressed it
to his throat.

Forever is a long time
to handle me
with care.

HAIKU: LOVE AFROS

braids fold nicely but
manipulation breaks strands
let's be wild and free

LOVE IS PATIENT

Love   plugs every hole with light
Love   birthed me and stayed
Love   carried the weight
Love   cringed in pain with me
Love   waited while I pushed it away
Love   was honest about what I deserved.
        And didn't.
Love   treated me
Love   comforted
Love   forgave
Love   endured
Love   listened
Love   sacrificed
Love   placed a girl from the hood with
        daddy/body/trust/trauma issues
        on a pedestal
Love   saved.

DELIGHT

Born in the shadows, pushed forth to light
I am my mother's and grandmother's delight
blanketed in ancient secrets and whispers
slept under arms forcing my whimpers
against devil's claws and voices shrill
I knew not the power of my own will.

Memories fade, but the body remembers
the burn of hot coal
the warmth of the embers
a shattered glass that fell unbroken
trusting tension lines won't burst open.

Gone are the fathers we'd never really know,
leaving holes for our burial
but seeds planted will grow.

MARVEL, A SUNFLOWER

From the dust, we emerge
rooted, standing tall,
brown at the center,
all sun around the outside.

In Hindsight

As I think back, it is quite a wonder
how inexplicably we have recovered
from bruise, from blunder, and life's fanged bite
from absence, and presence, in rooms teeming white.

I ponder on these things a lot
of will, of God, of strength to fight
of masks, of closets, of hidden things
of strategy, safety, and favored beings.

I know not why it goes this way
why tragedy precedes a sun-filled day
why from birth we kick and fight
why the roll before each flight?

I suppose it makes life much dearer
to see the cliffs in rearview mirrors
to eat our cake with bullets to bite
to have felt everything wrong
to know everything right.

BONUS MATERIAL

For book discussion questions and more, visit
www.nikki-murphy.com

RESOURCES

RAINN (Rape, Abuse & Incest National Network):
www.rainn.org

National Sexual Assault Telephone Hotline:
800-656-HOPE (4673)

National Suicide Prevention Lifeline:
800-273-8255

ABOUT THE AUTHOR

Nikki Murphy is an awarded Diversity & Inclusion Leader, real estate investor, poet and author. Born to high school sweethearts, she was raised by her mother in a home with extended family, including the many children her grandmother fostered over the years. Murphy is a native of Wyandanch, NY, a small, low-income, predominantly African-American community on Long Island.

She resides on Long Island with her husband and 4-year-old son.

Visit Nikki Murphy at www.nikki-murphy.com or @mrsnikkimurphy on Instagram and Twitter.

ACKNOWLEDGEMENTS

To my husband, Dana Murphy, thank you for everything—reading early manuscripts, encouraging me when I needed it most, taking care of everything when I needed the space to create, and for your loving patience as I navigate the emotional waters of my healing process. I am so blessed to do life with you.

To my son, Jaden Murphy, thank you for the love, urgency, and intentionality you brought into my life. I am a better woman, mother, child, wife, friend, and citizen because of the deep reflection and actions that you prompted me to engage in, so that you get the best version of me. I want the world for you, without limits and with the only expectation being to love and live well.

To my bonus son, Daisean Murphy, thank you for teaching me that love is not self-serving and for growing with me. I am so proud of the young man you are becoming.

To my mom, my rider, Doreen Lucas. I cannot thank you enough for raising me with love and teaching me resilience, independence and humor. You are the OG, the best to ever do it, single mom of every year, baddest motha alive. I love you and pray you keep living life and leaving it all on the dance floor. You keep me young!

To my nana in heaven, Ruby "Toni" Lucas, thank you for helping raise me, for always standing up for yourself and everybody else, for not caring what anyone thought about it, for not judging me, but also not allowing me to wallow in sorrow and for setting me straight when I need it. I have channeled your spirit heavily throughout this process. I couldn't have written this without you.

To my uncle, Darryl Lucas, for the lessons, the jokes, the incentives to do my best, and for being the first consistent male figure in my life.

To my family, the Lucas Gang, for the love, the fights, the laughter, and the space to cut up: Konstanz Lucas, Sunubia Lucas, David Lucas, Dwyde Lucas II, Dwyde Lucas III b.k.a Shy, Dah'Vielle Lucas, Divaahd Lucas, Daviana Lucas, James Brown, Audrey Brown, Nazir McLamb, Sha'Quel Jordan, and Chalin Scott. For growing up with one half of my family, y'all made it feel real full. A true blessing.

Love to my wonderful tribe—Taina Sanon, Shawnte Brown, Eliana Boyd, Angela Jennings, Tracy Barbot, Nathalie Vil, Esther Desvallons, Jennifer Lino, Danerys Gutierrez, Joanna Arredondo, Denysha Davis, Diana Rivera, Aracely Shildkret, Cecile Noble, Keisha Israel, Jennifer Saulino, Elizabeth Rine, Nicole Verheek, Lindsey Granger, Lauren Granger—for the encouragement, prayers, shares and real life support you all have given me before, to and through the publication of this book.

To my father in heaven, Randy Williamson, thank you for your honesty in that last conversation. We all are deeply human and never too far gone for redemption. Thank you for demonstrating this.

To everyone reading this and to all the Black people across the world, I love y'all deep.

Last, but never least, thank you Jesus for showing me love, grace and mercy. I pray it flows through me to everyone I touch, continually.

CPSIA information can be obtained
at www.ICGtesting.com
Printed in the USA
LVHW040834091120
671123LV00008B/225